Author's Note

I'm a poet, and I'm not going to let this world make me something I'm not. I'm not a grocery bagger. I'm not a shopping cart pusher. I'm not hosing down carts at a golf course. I'm not a sailor. I'm a poet.

Nicholas Leonard

UNSEEN ANGELS. The fountains in the Afterlove
awoke

with stretching crystal arms and beady yawns.
The water scratched against the marble stone
as angels passed with nurse-uniforms on.
Bizarre the scent of such an atmosphere;
the blown-out candles spun with sunscreen's tang.
Their children laughed aromas everywhere,
so morning mocked a summer night again.
Designed with plates of ivory on the walls,
the rows of angels' houses mourned the past.
With curving shingles topping each and all,
the villa pondered when Love would come back.
Again, the Afterlove began its day
where broken-hearts arrived to heal or stay.

3

UNSEEN ANGELS. Where July dwelled, its fleeting smell;

a romance made of smoke and mist.

Celebratory fires sprout

and wake to chase the sunblock's kiss.

Their scents collide with zinc and ash,

and crash against the sand where sunblock's sprayed.

Her tangy chill, her smoky groom;

they run away before they can be caught.

They run before they can be caught.

His burning suit, her ivory veil.

The summer's doomed to flee like lovers' star-crossed.

Avoidantary romance tale,

they run away before they can be caught.

They run before they can be caught.

UNSEEN ANGELS. The straw of blond was paling on his
head.
A dusty filter covered everything
as Franco squirmed and wriggled on the bed,
cradled in a snow-shaded straight jacket.
The ivory bricks inside the room were stale.
A room as cramped as that was smothering.
The only hope he saw was that gray door,
staring at him, watching, waiting, freezing.
Confused and flustered, not a movement worked.
His arms remained padlocked against his chest
throughout his fidgets that ribbited words
which chains and latches sing through now and then.
Stranded in the sable noir filter,
Franco felt surviving logic wither.

FRANCO. The hospital. The doctors failed
at prying final words from me.
Inadequacy's last exhale;
a plea mistook for misery.
My empty palm. My orphan art,
and left inside my room no one will see.
The gurney's rush. My urgent gush;
a leaking burst of poems I'll never write.
A leak of poems I'll never write.
My crimson ink. The wedding ring.
Everything I loved was doused in tears I cried.
I failed my wish. And scholars miss
my leaking burst of poems I'll never write.
A leak of poems I'll never write.

FRANCO. As parties halve, no parties stop,
and suits are just as flat as pelts.
Unexpectedly prices drop.
They're sold to suit somebody else.
A limping hope. A bowing head,
exhausted underneath a stoic stress.
As answers halve, the studies rise.
No angel asks where have the groomsmen gone.
And where have all the groomsmen gone?
The others shrug, "what about us?"
The questions asked and the conversations done,
so sure they'll leave asylum ruts.
No angel asks where have the groomsmen gone.
And where have all the groomsmen gone?

UNSEEN ANGELS. His ears avoid an angel's voice.
She asks him what he did for work.
An allegedly lazy choice:
the art he made was just ignored.
A crusted brush. They turn and hush,
before they flood his room with stethoscopes.
They'll brag about him later on.
Hear the angels talk about the artist?
Angels talk about the artist.
He followed heart, and picked his art
instead of working like a capitalist.
It's art which makes the misers starve.
Hear the angels talk about the artist?
Angels talk about the artist.

CAMILLA. His art is art nobody ever saw.
Too hard to park their eye upon a book,
his counterparts perceived his path bizarre.
And artists rot because their art's unlooked.
Viola, did you see his timid glare?
Where then I brushed his arm by accident,
a shy apology was in his stare.
It made him pause his twisting on the bed;
the twist of grieving starry starry nights.
VIOLA. I think his pain is caused by bride betrayal.
We weren't employed to heal his artly plight.
We'll heal the bite which came behind the veil.
CAMILLA. I'll tell him that his art is not extinct,
though purgatory's prime for posthumists.

GENEVA. Narcissus Ward has passed inspection day
with little gripe to hear from royal lips,
and now the queen is out along her way
to check the Widow Ward where widows sit.
Our gardens never stray from being green.
Despite our patient's faces, flowers bloom
because we know their pain will one day cease.
It ceased before for other patients too.
Our patients just require longer stays
because their trauma bonds just last so long,
and gaslit candlesticks are hard to tame.
And nonetheless, these souls learn to move on,
except the one we got this yesterday.
Is Franco in a better state today?

VIOLA. We heard his heart confess to stethoscopes,
though can't translate the things its beat confessed.
GENEVA. They're not his sins his spirit should atone.
And that's the hum you heard beneath his chest.
His cure is in our tolerance and help.
And after Franco's soul is cleansed of hurt,
he can transcend to Heaven or to Hell.
CAMILLA. This boy, his soul's destined for Heaven's
court.
VIOLA. Perhaps, you'll find this not informative.
Entrancing smiles often hide their fangs.
His bride's were sheathed until they pierced his skin.
Too deep inside his Love, he let them stay.
GENEVA. He could believe we also hide a pair,
alike a skeptic puppy; skittish, scared.

GENEVA. His case has signs of moral injury.
Her scold evoked his puppy-heart to dent
til dames appeared as rival enemies;
if Romeo refused fair Juliet.
"I love you, Franco." What a dreadful lie.
A caring man with all his trust betrayed
will drive his lips to drink the reddest wine.
If one was false the others must be fake.
Her knife was just too handsome in his back.
It broke his balance, then his morals limped
throughout his falter on his morals' track,
too hurt to ever trust and love again.
CAMILLA. You say this statement so remorselessly.
VIOLA. The way a soldier names a casualty.

GENEVA. A blemished map is what directs his soul.
A soul without a place to go will rust
until it's green as Hamlet's father's ghost.
So, healing Franco Finnegan's a must.
His every path for light has lost appeal
because her bridal light became a void
by treating hearts alike a thing to steal.
And sable silence seems his only choice.
CAMILLA. He loved with all his heart allowed to give.
It gave with willing wonder, free and loose
until betrayal destroyed its chariot;
upon the floor ignored by fleeing hooves.
GENEVA. Our white aprons will wipe away his tears
until his soul commutes to some elsewhere.

UNSEEN ANGELS. As petals shed, he bowed his head
to mourn a Love he thought was real.
Penitentiary took him in,
where angels help them rest and heal.
Narcissus Wing, they checked him in
where angels dressed as nurses rush to work.
As apology letters burned
they tucked a drooping rose between his lips.
They tucked a rose between his lips.
Though richly green, the stem was weak
as straight-jacket's locks re-clicked like wedding rings.
Ministering him therapy,
they tucked a drooping rose between his lips.
They tucked a rose between his lips.

UNSEEN ANGELS. The angels hushed. The angels
watched
their patients skulk where palmleaves grow.
Observatory angels stopped
behind the railings made of stone.
Their timid steps. Their bowing heads.
Asylum gardens drank its yellow light
where sunlight asked how leaves were green
while the angels watched him mourn romance.
The angels watched him mourn romance.
They feld their arms to hear him talk
where shrubs and hedges allowed his voice to land.
Confessionary speech was caught
because the angels watched him mourn romance.
The angels watched him mourn romance.

FRANCO. With fake remorse, her tears were forced
and dressed in black and white I sleeped.
Obituary photos warned
with smiles that I used to beam.
Her fibbing mouth, it feld a frown
but she's relieved because nobody knew.
Despite her seated at the front,
she knows I lived without an honest kiss.
I lived without an honest kiss.
My ivory clay. They bow and pray
with so much to see behind my closed eyelids.
And Venus had nothing to say
because I lived without an honest kiss.
I lived without an honest kiss.

CAMILLA. He's grim again amongst the greenery.

I hate to hear him say these things again,

reciting thoughts about his tragedy.

VIOLA. As bags below his eyes refuse to dim.

CAMILLA. His eyes are still rewatching letters burn.

VIOLA. They wait for flames to eat the rose he holds.

How could this be a thing a man deserves?

CAMILLA. Within romance, the fire's all he's known.

I feel a quilt of guilt begin to fall

because we stand and watch throughout his speech.

VIOLA. I say we should remain silent for now.

CAMILLA. But his speech makes the rose's health

decrease.

Perhaps we should assist and pause his pain

before his wary lashes spark a flame.

Paramours plan his Love's funeral.

VIOLA. I say we let him feel his doom for now.

FRANCO. With forceful weeps, the truth's retrieved.
She tells me that she faked it all.
Monogamy dies in its sleep;
paramours plan the funeral.
Women and men; they all pretend
to mourn its death before their parties start
as angels dragged me far away.
Alone, I asked if Love'll stay alive.
I asked if Love'll stay alive.
Where stardust dwelled, they checked my pulse,
and work was done upon my vampire bite.
Their tweezers' pull, my twisted shout.
Alone, I asked if Love'll stay alive.
I asked if Love'll stay alive.

CAMILLA. Oh, now he does a new eternal nod
and stirs the pot of pity in my chest
as bachelor eyes search the clouds who flock
with lies of hope above his craning neck.
VIOLA. I think the cloud who ferries Love has passed.
CAMILLA. Oh, stall and halt my mouth before I shout
to tell him that his cloud will ferry back.
Oh, sweet-daydreaming boy, depart from doubt.
VIOLA. We should debate an action on his state.
The order's that we watch, and watched we did.
So, let's record this scene instead of stay.
CAMILLA. Oh, let me stay to hear another wish.
The clouds ignore him, but I won't ignore
as Franco wishes out forevermore.

FRANCO. With fingers thin, and diamond nails
they dangle daintly off a cloud.
Illusionary hope, prevail!
and say when my One will come down.
A reaching hand, a hopeful glance
before the wind demands the clouds to move
until the birches let me back
wherefore I dream about an angel's wrist.
I dream about an angel's wrist.
I hold my head, my palms instead
and worry that my angel might not exist.
Abandonary flowerbed,
wherefore I dream about an angel's wrist.
I dream about an angel's wrist.

NEVERRIA. Your eyelids blink the way a flower bows.
Your lashes sink and raise through lakes of hurt;
persistent that they'll swim to reach the ground
where water tugs its tired roots no more.
FRANCO. Your hand has swiped apart the wall of pine.
And like a hand is patient on a pond,
it waits atop the water's skin for mine?
NEVERRIA. To take your drifting hand before it drowns.
FRANCO. Your eyes have grabbed me first before your
hand.
They give me hope and fuel and joy to swim
to fingers that'll keep me on the land,
where eyes'll meet a thousand times again.
NEVERRIA. So let our nearly meeting fingers meet.
Before the flood of angels let us leave.

UNSEEN ANGELS. Without alert, her hand emerged
and eager joy was on her face.
Indocuary fingers curled
around his own which stretched awake.
Her closing hand, its dainty pull.
How could the garden-wall ignore her face?
Her growing smirk. It froze the warmth
as shrubs pretended not to see their sprint.
The shrubs forgot to stop their sprint.
Her waiting stance, their meeting glance,
that collided in the garden labyrinth;
impactuary like their hands.
The shrubs pretended not to see their sprint.
The shrubs forgot to stop their sprint.

UNSEEN ANGELS. With sweetened smoke, her palace
dozed
where torches grilled the flavor off
imperially white limestone.
The smell cologned the Afterlove.
An ember glow, as pillars flexed
with palace floors appearing smooth and paved.
Affairs between the smoke and clouds;
they smelled the torches overcook the dark.
The torches overcooked the dark.
A sandy quartz, its gleam rehearsed
where pillars guarded where golden shadows parked.
The angels had their spot reserved
where they smelled torches overcook the dark.
The torches overcooked the dark.

UNSEEN ANGELS. Two angels walked with echoed heels
below the canopy of clouds.
With tranquility on their trail,
they hushed along the lustered grounds.
Adorning red, adorning white,
adorning colors that Adonis donned,
the angels neared the pillars' rank.
They came with mouths about to speak with verse.
With mouths about to speak with verse.
The darkest blue, an orange hue.
The only angels upon the roofless court
betweened the night and torches' youth.
They came with mouths about to speak with verse.
With mouths about to speak with verse.

CAMILLA. You know, I passed his room this afternoon.

VIOLA. And did you catch nostalgia on your way?

CAMILLA. I saw the flash of doom his eyes assumed
the day his paining heart was sprung awake.

VIOLA. Despite the talk, I fear it stays the same.

CAMILLA. Viola, dear, I think you judge too soon.

VIOLA. You saw a shadow which I fear remains?

CAMILLA. An empty room. No one inside the room.
You worry much the way an angel shan't.

VIOLA. Our honor's wrapped in worried sonatas.
We just rewrite the music that is damp
until the wind of worries flee operas.

CAMILLA. And we'll do our duties in different do's.
Perhaps our queen has found her own to do.

UNSEEN ANGELS. Anubis envied Neverria's house.
The truth is that she knew this truth was fact,
so did the torches lining every wall.
The Egyptians wanted their style back.
Although an underworld of temples slept,
her house was deep alive and deep awake.
Her house was that remnant of temple flesh
where angel footsteps paced to renovate.
Orange twilight conquered the corridors
as yestertorches made Anubis frown.
They ran their light along the marble floors
until the archaic allusions drowned.
With hearts forever doomed to crack or melt,
Anubis envied no other place else.

NEVERRIA. The tale cannot profane itself with words.
Oh, when I saw my Franco first appear,
in the gardens of the Narcissus Ward,
the clouds of Heaven begged to come live here.
And just how could I not've plucked him out?
and yanked him out from out between the ferns,
despite the angel-nurses' urgent shouts.
So quickly out those gardens did we lurch.
I'll let a lulling Love attend his Life
alike a lullaby he never heard.
These lullabies will be the ones I write
about the boy I saved from out the ward.
Oh, stop the past from haunting everyday.
Inside my Life my Love's forever safe.

NEVERRIA. Your gaze acryls its own achillic ache.
You aim your view to scrutinize your death.
You've paid your bill with less idyllic days,
so take your view and view your queen instead.
My palm's your heel, forever on your chest,
forbidding any enemy arrows.
So love and feel. Remember not regrets,
for sitting on your chest's my healing poem.
So let my gentle fingers guide your chin
until our eyes crusade a matching course
before this royal dinner-night begins.
Achilled, revived and safe. Believe my words.
My marvel's in his polar-ivory suit.
No longer stained with paint he used to use.

FRANCO. They want me in their world of strict routine.
Suggestions try to put me in their group.
"Another cog in the murder machine,"
I've never nor will ever break my rules.
NEVERRIA. My artist led a dedicated Life.
You lived, and now you're never going home.
An Aztec priestess loves a sacrifice,
ah, but you'll never see the altar's stone.
My hand and palm already hold your heart.
It's wasted in asylums where it dulls.
The world misused it, fueling greedy barks.
There's never any need to take it out.
Your drive has greater cut than any blade
and stops the systems that rewards its slaves.

FRANCO. My boutonniere's already on my chest.

NEVERRIA. You're saying that my hand is like a rose?

FRANCO. Your palm and flowers share a calming breath,
expelling air so that my breath's composed.

NEVERRIA. We know the strongest plant has roots of
five,
and matching plants together make a ten.
If plants with twenty roots forever thrive,
I'll plant my palms forever on you then.
A pair of different flowers bend to touch,
alike our fingers that are interlocked,
before they shed their petals on the mud.
Oh, but we won't untie our rooted knot.

FRANCO. We'll let the sun adore and see our roots?

NEVERRIA. Its light will watch us plant the Life we
choose.

FRANCO. Her eyelids wear the ocean's deepest tint;
created out from paint across her pores.
And pointing like the falcon's spreading wings.
The blue eyeshadow argues with her skin;
a peach a little darker than the floors
as her eyes wear the ocean's deepest tint.
The two triangles stretch perfectly twinned.
A pair of maelstrom clouds approach the shore.
They're pointing like the falcon's spreading wings.
And when her eyes daydream about her prince,
the blue almost decays above the pearls,
then her eyes aren't the ocean's deepest tint.
They flap whenever Neverria blinks,
and help her aim a spot where eyes'll soar.
They're pointing like the falcon's spreading wings.
Ignoring rumors that she knows are born,
reflecting flickers that jump torch to torch-
her eyelids wear the ocean's deepest tint,
and point like the falcon's spreading wings.

UNSEEN ANGELS. A hallway where eternity is vague;
two angels passed between the pillars' corps.
Geneva crossed her arms with locked complaint.
Her angst was masked as sweet Camilla smirked.
A pharaoh smiled in the shadows' tar,
expanding in his search for stolen gold.
A hallowed-while made the clock unstart.
He's damned to spend it cursed; a golden ghost.
The hall was dim and tanned with cleo thrills
because their queen exhausted every wall.
Her mouth emitted lines of novels spilt;
a pond of steep accounts about her Love.
It stained the pillars that were standing guard,
a shade of candle wax the fires charm.

GENEVA. Irresponsible fingers grabbed the wrong.
And now we trail his ragamuffin pace
where queens forget about the crowns they don,
and end where Neverria spends her days.
A giddy pace has plagued your feet, fair nurse.
You leap alike a reaper late for work,
who now is catching up behind the hearse.
CAMILLA. Oh, but we've never seen this grave before!
I skip because I think we'll see his joy.
Romantic rumors wrap these pillars now!
They're what his lovesick dreams always employed.
You've never seen him wish upon a cloud.
Why not allow the Afterlove a king?
GENEVA. You clearly don't know Franco Finnegan.

CAMILLA. I watched him every morning in the maze,
between the hedges underneath the ledge,
where roses droop because they loathed his gaze.
They bent to hear the ground's silence instead.
Oh, but I stood above him, listening
as angels dressed as nurses rushed and worked
before the queen arrived with swiftened hands
during my watch upon the marble porch.
GENEVA. How did he catch our queen's unbowing eye?
So sure about the patient that she stole,
she writes with pencils that believe they're knives,
who say my disagreement's disallowed.
Her duty's never been to love a man.
Let's stop the crown from falling onto him.

CAMILLA. He won't become a thief who takes the crown.

GENEVA. Oh, but a wedding may present him half
if Neverria wears a wedding gown.

CAMILLA. The crown? You think he's only after that?

GENEVA. My friend, remember what our ward entails!
Narcissists play the victim cleverly.
How do we know he loves our queen for real?
He could be fooling her with poetry.

CAMILLA. The boy is not narcissistic a bit.
This miracle of Love is not a front.
Besides, remember interviewing him?
He's sweet and wants nothing except true Love.

GENEVA. I'm skeptical because this is our queen.
Coincidence it wasn't you or me.

UNSEEN ANGELS. Before the guests arrived to dine,
his face became her fingers' path.
Caffeinationry calming eyes
reread the razor's aftermath.
His cooling face, she dropped her gaze
to see the petals spread their scarlet sheets.
Against his white and ivory suit,
she put her palace rose against his chest.
She put a rose against his chest.
Her blink reserved a later course
which would lead her fingers further down his neck.
It pricked his suit alike a thorn
as his queen put a rose against his chest.
She put a rose against his chest.

NEVERRIA. I should've warned before about our guest.
The nurse Geneva said our Love's unreal.
She's said so in her letters that protest.
Tonight, we'll watch her wrong opinions peel.
A hearing ear will never shun a flute.
Our sheet of music rivers long the sky
whose speckled streets of wonder teaches you.
I see you study that inside your eyes.
Our eyes will watch Geneva's arms uncross
before her lips uncross to start debate.
Tonight we can disband the thing she thought
because our cosmic Love's motif will play.
Before she can begin her vain protest,
our Love will strip the dining room of breath.

FRANCO. My heartbeat's dash: it's vote is cast
to make asylums crumble down.
No purgatories take me back
because I'm in your palace now.
Our royal dawn has just begun.
She's just another shadow in a chair
who's never heard a suite so tuned.
Tonight she'll hear our cosmic Love's motif.
She'll hear our cosmic Love's motif.
The inky night has teaching tides,
where sand awakes to learn the stars' twinkled beat;
universally scratch and chime.
Tonight she'll hear our cosmic Love's motif.
She'll hear our cosmic Love's motif.

UNSEEN ANGELS. A starting course. Excitement surged
with silent bolts from out her eyes.
Possessionary gleeful smirk;
she aimed it down the row of wine.
Without a word, her rule prevailed
by that demand she twinkled in her eyes.
With sturdy lash, and scarab black,
her eyes appeared to proudly own the world.
Her eyes appeared to own the world.
As tables crowned themselves with plates,
her looking seemed to charm the slithering smoke.
Nobility- her resting face.
Her eyes appeared to proudly own the world.
Her eyes appeared to own the world.

GENEVA. His grief has ran and weakened, so I hear?

He was so glum amongst asylum shrubs.

NEVERRIA. With leashing hands, I lead him everywhere.

We've traveled in exhausts of nighttime's hush.

I've made him chuckle in our hasty tour.

Geneva, what a sweetened antidote!

to trade his sorrow in for happy chords.

A sweeter shanty's never got to float.

CAMILLA. I'd love to spectate such a marathon,

and watch the bounce of running silhouettes.

NEVERRIA. The doves have less a stellar flight to flaunt

contrast to how we run with thrilling steps.

FRANCO. My queen has sweetness that has banned my

woe.

NEVERRIA. And sweetened shanties only get to float.

NEVERRIA. Geneva, where has dear Viola gone?

GENEVA. She felt a tug upon vocation's leash,

and scurried back to work to catch a thought.

NEVERRIA. Forever drawn to chase free-thinking leaves.

She fuels herself with honor, that I think.

I've heard its proud exhaust rejuve her voice

the times she's read me the departure list.

CAMILLA. Oh please. Her honor's been her only choice.

NEVERRIA. Ah! Anyways, be seated, everyone.

FRANCO. What's for dinner?

NEVERRIA. I had them make your dino nuggets, hun.

CAMILLA. And, uh, what's the kind of wine tonight?

GENEVA. I think I've lost my interest in the wine.

I want to take this dinner in soberly;

recalling strange occasions orderly.

NEVERRIA. You've met Geneva, right, Franco darling?

FRANCO. Yes.

NEVERRIA. Also fair Camilla on her right?

FRANCO. Yes.

CAMILLA. Neverria, why's the wine orange?

NEVERRIA. It came from villas donned with mango
vines.

GENEVA. Perhaps introductions aren't yet complete.

This now, I'm putting Franco on the spot.

So, Franco Finnegan, so stand and speak.

So speak and let the cork of stories pop.

We've had a lot of games of cat and mouse,

and yet I've never caught your total tale.

Explain your time of when the earth you dwelled.

Profess of better times your soul prevailed.

My ears are thirsty in your weird silence,

and yearn for stories that you could present.

FRANCO. As class resumed, I wrote and drew
on a test marked with scarlet ink.
Equationary boredom flew
above my restless pencil prints.
A teaching sigh, constrict-comply.
I begged the bell to love me back for good.
With Gatsby's death, we read MacBeth
and then the auditorium collapsed.
The auditorium collapsed.
A passing grade, mayor's handshake
before I walked away with proof that I passed.
Academicly end of days;
I felt the auditorium collapse.
The auditorium collapsed.

CAMILLA. Oh! Tell about your friends!

FRANCO. On Saturdays, the sunlight strained,

and down on us its yellow poured

like ordinary lemonade

we drank before we built our fort.

A sleepover, a sci-fi film

that had a "scary" part we'd fast-forward.

Then we'd pretend we fled through space

as we slid down the spiral yellow slide.

We rode the spiral yellow slide.

We ran around, and jumped and bounced,

as the couch became a spaceship in our minds.

With joyous shouts, we twisted down,

as we slid down the spiral yellow slide.

We rode the spiral yellow slide.

FRANCO. "Be good and sit," they told the kids,
"we'll come and get you if you stray."
Distractionary politics.
The greedy cycle masquerades.
With 9 to 5's, the art'll die
if artists find themselves inside the mill.
Ingenuity's casket shuts
and locks until the Man is Man again.
Until the Man is Man again.
A busy man forgets to live
inside the factory full of mannequins.
Despite the rules, I boldly quit
to paint until the Man is Man again.
Until the Man is Man again.
GENEVA. I'm sure they loved you.

FRANCO. By fireside, I packed my eyes
as night surrounded forest's crib.
With cemetery thoughts revived,
I shared my tale with firepits.
A Sam Cooke song, a subtle crack,
so soft enough to let the pine gossip.
Extraordinary chilling warmth,
I'd think until the embers learned my name.
Until the embers learned my name.
My thoughts were loud. Their tempest wail.
And eyelashes fell to fan the fainting flames.
They saw my tale. It made them frail.
I'd think until the embers learned my name.
Until the embers learn my name.

FRANCO. As morning croaked, my brushes stroked
and asked which ear I'd sever first.
My purgatory studio
where paintings died upon their birth.
Romantic twists, my mental kiss
I left on the portrait for them to see.
Rejectionary timid *thanks.*
They knew I'd hang before my paintings do.
I'd hang before my paintings do.
My sunken gaze, my stubbled face
as scratching bristles spread the color blue.
They took my razor blades away.
They knew I'd hang before my paintings do.
I'd hang before my paintings do.
CAMILLA. Can we hear a poem?
FRANCO. No.
It's up to the people on Earth to read them now.
NEVERRIA. A love for art is weightless gold.
The workers work to fill their purse
as artists make their art to pay their soul.
FRANCO. I know who meets the reaper first.

NEVERRIA. A twinkle's rung somewhere because he's
sighed,
and reapers want to hunt his hooveless breath.
Unriddle what you fear, and awe my eyes,
and give a chance for calming looks to vex.
So silent, silent boy, my silent boy.
They'll never stop your stampeding of dreams.
Inside protective palaces rejoice.
I built a dreaming bridge. It leads to me.
You'll only see me in a nightly gown,
and never skeletons with scythes and cloaks.
No bony hand will take you from me now.
Depression's biggest fear is angel's gold.
This new affection rides eternally
with dust behind ourselves to blind the grief.

NEVERRIA. To Franco!

FRANCO. Forget the wine! Forget the wine!

I'd rather taste your swishing lips.

Some drinks will leave a poisoned bite.

Your lips will never strike me sick.

As light retreats this dinner feast,

and lips arrest these glasses' crystal shores,

my lips demand they stay alert

because my lips await your glassless mouth.

My lips await your glasseless mouth.

Forget my toast. Forget my toast.

My lips pucker shut; prepared for something else.

My sober lips will drink the most

because my lips await your glassless mouth.

My lips await your glassless mouth.

GENEVA. To Franco.

NEVERRIA. Aw!

He blushes like a timid tomato.

And red's a color that I must follow.

CAMILLA. If only music mimed their chemistry.

Relief is hammocked underneath his eyes

with jolly cruises eyes attend to see;

to see his damage funds the sweetest sigh.

GENEVA. It's punk disguised as true and honest pop.

He breeds a wonder that allures our queen.

Her fun is eyeing gloom she thinks she stops

as grief is under what appears is sweet.

CAMILLA. I hear the thunder mime the pianos-

GENEVA. I hear no thunder on this scenic night.

CAMILLA. Because it runs wherever they go.

GENEVA. Camilla, hear yourself. Your speech is high.

There's not a music note inside this room.

CAMILLA. Because they left to write a note anew.

VIOLA. I wonder what twilight his flame survived?
I watch its fire's up and down parade;
repeating every dive and rise and dive
to look for Hell and Heaven everyday.
His soul deserves a timely chance to heal.
And yet it's in the palace and not here.
My most austere and weirdest patient yet.
His need for staying in here should be clear!
Perhaps our queen is just ignorant now,
and swept away with vain affection's thrill;
forgetting what an angel swears and vows.
Throughout the speech of kisses lust does quill.
I wonder what she saw in him to love,
which broke the rule which says angels cannot.

FRANCO. A stem syringe. My chest is pricked.
The ivy stem vacuums my blood.
Parasitically ivy drip;
hydrating petals back to health.
Its caring touch. I'm pale enough
as my suit obtains zero crimson stains
because the thorn; it takes the red,
injecting color in the final rose.
Injecting color in the rose.
My vein adheres. It takes its share;
small amounts so that I don't become a ghost
Injectionary boutonniere,
injecting color in the final rose.
Injecting color in the rose.

VIOLA. Franco! I've made a grave discovery.
Her vain affection's just a clever mask.
Her love is just unwaning vanity.
This reign of hot excitement's doomed to pass.
You can't believe the things she says to you,
no matter just how safe and sweet she'll sound.
A queen desires trophies, gold and jewels.
Although my queen adorns a sacred crown,
she may obey an ancient mortal greed.
Return to that Narcissus Ward you fled.
Validation! Vanity, vexes she!
Return to us, and wait there for Heaven.
You just excite her like a diamond's song;
only shining in the eye for so long.

FRANCO. I pause to dread, her Love's pretend,
and wonder what it is she wants.
Cynically I bow my head
and rub my brow with pensive thought.
Her calming gaze, my yesterdays;
they ask to dance with quick and nervous looks.
She puts my hand below her eye.
Perhaps her face has not a mask to lift?
Her face has not a mask to lift.
Our masquerade, my anxious wait
where I feel my heart try not to wince and flinch-
until she tells me that I'm safe.
Perhaps her face has not a mask to lift?
Her face has not a mask to lift.

NEVERRIA. My cinnamon!

You look exhausted.

FRANCO. Too much to think about,

NEVERRIA. Think about what?

FRANCO. What do you think about me?

NEVERRIA. What do you mean?

FRANCO. Do you love me?

NEVERRIA. With all my heart.

Do you love me?

FRANCO. Do I love you?

NEVERRIA. Profess! Profess! Profess!

Propel the truth from out thy chest.

FRANCO. Of course I do,

because you open my heart without a key.

NEVERRIA. There's not a lock nor chain around our

Love.

Like birds who had escaped their cage to flee,

with wings, our Love forever skips the clouds.

So let Love's confession fly around me!

with subtle landing pauses on my mouth.

FRANCO. I love you!

NEVERRIA. And land.

They kiss.

NEVERRIA. Now Franco,

why did you ask about my Love for you?

FRANCO. One of the angels said you're using me.

NEVERRIA. Who?

Franco.

Who?

FRANCO. Viola.

NEVERRIA. What?

Did you believe her?

FRANCO. No. Of course not.

She was stubborn and convincing.

She spoke as if she was right,

and if she was wrong she would make it come true just to be

right.

NEVERRIA. I thought she would be happy for us.

How did you respond?

FRANCO. I ran away.

NEVERRIA. And came to me?

FRANCO. Yes.

NEVERRIA. Be faithful in the pen you call my tongue.
I'll never need a drop of ink to speak.
Imagine what I'll sign with words to come,
and know I vow to write no tragedy.
Admit my voice is scratching on your chest,
and writing lyrics deep below your skin.
Your heart's a book with so much story left,
with hieroglyphics begging to get in.
I know there's always something new to write.
We'll drivel this iambic speech we learn.
Despite the river that brings Life to Night,
your skin won't wrinkle like the letters burn.
We'll find a torch and study the tomb's walls
as dreadful dust from yesterday dissolves.
FRANCO. I believe you.
Tell me what to do.
NEVERRIA. Be mine.

UNSEEN ANGELS. With hands enjoined, she pulled her
boy.
The mattress caught their aerial.
Collisionary lips rejoiced
amongst their bells of cardio.
A safe impact. Her cageless laugh.
 It swept tattoos she never asked about.
The hours' dust. A ticking broom.
Her grin, it made his purgatory stop.
She made his purgatory stop.
With royal charm, asylums fade.
They laid together with eye contact prolonged;
solidarity face to face.
Her grin, it made his purgatory stop.
She made his purgatory stop.

NEVERRIA. I've trained endangered lips to land on mine.

FRANCO. My lips have flown a desperate search for you.

NEVERRIA. No greater raptor's ever got to glide,

because you own the vastest surf of blue.

I know you flew beyond the height they warned.

Ah, but you're not another Icarus,

because so few abscond against the herd-

you stayed upon you hunt for vividness.

The wind protests below determined wings.

Ah, but you sliced a cut between the clouds.

FRANCO. I wish they craned their necks before I sinked,

and shuttled down into the sea to drown.

NEVERRIA. Although you sunk, you never switched

your course.

I know the spot your wings were meant to perch.

FRANCO. These fingers that caress my face are soap,

and wash the sorrow stuck within my pores.

They sting with what empresses' ache to own;

a touch you borrowed straight from July's shores.

NEVERRIA. I hold a beach the world forgot to map.

Ah, let empresses envy angel hands.

They've faulted where my fingers want to nap.

I get to trek this country where lips land.

FRANCO. The further that these fingers tour my face,

the further that my soul is owned by you.

NEVERRIA. My favorite track my fingers tour and trace;

my favorite tracks' the smiles owned by you.

And let your fingers go explore as well.

There's more to own the more our fingers dwell.

FRANCO. With bathing done, the stars are lost.
They cling and hide against your skin
as Aphrodite's ocean dawn
is put to shame after our swim.
You stand and stare. My begging glare.
You take my breath the way you stole the stars
I've seen the snow pretend to shine
the way there twinkles diamonds on my muse.
There twinkles diamonds on my muse.
The waters' stained. Its drops remain,
and weaves a lacy gown of slick crystal dew.
Illuminary bodyscape;
it's where there twinkles diamond on my muse.
There twinkles diamonds on my muse.

NEVERRIA. Maroon me on the chest I often stroke.

No rush. My boy, can we forever drift?

Canoes have on the dresses coffins know,

ah, but my buoyant artist never sinks.

FRANCO. Your magnet heart forbids the water's greed.

It's tethering us two upon this bed.

Our magnets share a blissly tempered beat.

I'll never sink with you upon my chest.

NEVERRIA. I hope the shore of morning's far away,

and that the sleeping sun forgets to hail.

FRANCO. This moment's shortened course will scar the
waves,

for memory will not forget our trail.

NEVERRIA. And smoothly like we sail the indigo-

ah, foolish time. I wish its pace to slow.

FRANCO. I'm in the scene I wish I learned to paint.
A muse who's sprawled atop her tired bard,
within the room where kisses detonate
to bruise the walls and dark with brighter charm.
They're painting one another in their minds
with dueling eyes exciting tired air-
NEVERRIA. The lake's begun its falter in your eyes
to move the tides where goddesses appear.
I see your eyes reflect her radiance.
It adds phenomenal amounts of care
as breeze arrives to test this ambience
and adds its natural amount of flair.
FRANCO. My muse is decorating every eye,
and proves the best of paintings stem from Life.

UNSEEN ANGELS. His weakened blink, her teasing grin,
and face to face upon the sheets.
Synchronizingly eyelids dipped
as memories began their lease.
His consciousness was rolled away
alike the storm's reluctance in its end.
Her scholar glare, it watched him drift
as both their resting eyes prepared to nap.
Their resting eyes prepared to nap.
A soothing breeze applauded sleep.
The warmth escaped and the clouds reflected that.
Despite the gusts, they wouldn't freeze
as both their resting eyes prepared to nap.
Their resting eyes prepared to nap.

CAMILLA. Ah, when his speeches swam above the green.
Attempting not to drown, he reached for clouds.
Her hand; a frog. His hand; a floating leaf.
His hand is safe with Neverria now.
The weirdest beauty bit my patient ear
throughout my time upon the ledge above.
Oh, wishes trail again the atmosphere!
Oh, but nobody wishes like he does.
He knew the thing he sought amongst his Hell
the time the wind demanded clouds to move.
He never thought to look beside himself.
Perhaps my queen was listening too.
The clock was slower in a wishful week
the days I heard her Franco wish for she.

GENEVA. Today is not your rose's funeral.

WINCHESTA. It's crisp with age and blackened like a
wick.

CAMILLA. I hold the one her Franco tuned to bow.

His garden speeches kept this flower lit.

GENEVA. You think he prophesied this royal Love?

CAMILLA. He wished for Love, and Love he got.

GENEVA. Enough.

Our partisan of coven angels meet

before her fling becomes a dire scene.

The highest-ranking angels left their wards

and gather in these gardens here to talk.

Winchesta left the Ghosted Ward to speak.

As well as Ariel from the Paramour Ward.

Willow from the Widow Ward.

Eden from the Ward of the Dumped.

ARIEL. Why do we meet here?

GENEVA. To make decisions on our queen's romance.

VIOLA. Be wary on deciding what to do.

There's not a key which can unlock her arms.

Her arms will flex and fight to keep her groom.

I know. I've seen her hold him in a hug.

WINCHESTA. The queen forgot to sign a name this week

upon this coming week's departure list,

and now an extra week this patient stays

an extra week inside my Ghosted Ward.

Oh, but my patients learned to wait

because the pending grey bewitched their days,

and haunted during mortal days of wait.

And now our queen has ghosted this patient.

VIOLA. I wish I could've caught this grim mistake.

I read our queen the list the night before.

She did appear distracted in the daze

throughout my reading in the corridor.

WINCHESTA. This patient thought she was supposed to leave.

She spent the night upon the floor with tears,

the same she must've cried the night he left

without a word, without explanation.

GENEVA. This could occur to all our patients, friends.

I plea you think about your patients' souls.

Our queen's behavior must remain alert,

and not admiring with bachelors.

ARIEL. And this is true?

GENEVA. We saw it at her dinner last evening.

She's cheating on her royal duties,

and cheating like the men who chaught the hearts

your ward is filled with, Ariel.

Her love for order's fled

and landed on her Franco Finnegan.

He's just another paramour;

another ill-intended bachelor.

VIOLA. *(whispering to Camilla)*

No longer mourn the rose, Camilla.

Geneva's got support from every villa.

And hold your tongue, friend.

This Love deserves an early end.

CAMILLA. But she loves him!

GENEVA. A queen shall not require any king.

It's men who make the bright dynasties dim.

ARIEL. What's proposed?

GENEVA. A trial of impeachment.

Our patients' lunch is close to ending now.

We must discuss this later.

VIOLA. Whose words invited such a wary frown?
You're not the way you look and often seem.
CAMILLA. These petals write obituaries now
because they overheard the angels scheme.
VIOLA. A flower can't conjure a graveyard verse.
It's bent because it's died by nature's law,
and law is what will pave our honor's course!
so leave the rose upon the soil's lawn.
CAMILLA. This flower learned to write because he spoke.
It writes its feelings in the air we smell.
I smell its plea for hope begin to mold
because you lott inject their Love with doubt.
VIOLA. Camilla, drop the rose and flee its fume.
I think its lying toxins poisoned you.

UNSEEN ANGELS. The morning roved with mellow gold
pretending that it wouldn't pale.
Hibernationry nuzzled pose;
they laid as curtains flapped and sailed.
A peaceful face. Their shuddered gaze
as balconies invited lemon light.
Nirvaniary bedroom pause.
They laid and leisured in their lazy nap.
They leisured in their lazy nap.
A subtle breeze, it watched them sleep
as reeds played the songs the palace wanted back.
Residuary solar gleam.
They laid and leisured in their lazy nap.
They leisured in their lazy nap.

UNSEEN ANGELS. Below her yawn, she rolled her palm
across his shyly built bicep.
Expeditionry fingers marched,
and smoothed the skin of their conquest.
Addictive pace. She traced a vein
with speed the plow obeys upon the mud.
He flexed his arm. She laughed and teased,
and lay, awaiting goosebumps that'd sprout.
Awaiting goosebumps that'd sprout.
With tidal speed, and back and forth
she waved her hand to pet his vanilla pelt.
Inquisitory fingers worked.
Her pat; awaiting goosebumps that'd sprout.
Awaiting goosebumps that'd sprout.

NEVERRIA. Destiny's blanket covers both our chests.
Awaking underneath is such a thrill.
It's phantom drank no better dose of breath
than what's exhaled across these sheets and silk.
I dreamed and thought we'd frolic in a reeds,
to catch more fate and bring it back to bed.
If Venus helped Adonis catch the beast,
perhaps he'd stay her prince forever then.
FRANCO. I'll hunt nothing except a day with you.
NEVERRIA. I'll flee and make you chase me in the field,
and after that we'll laugh and stop the noon
before its tint begins to waste its peel.
The morning sky demands we run for fun,
so let's explore an odder place to lounge.

UNSEEN ANGELS. A solar yolk, its sunlight cracked.
They ran throughout the yellow reeds.
Midasuary blades of grass
applauded on their busy knees.
A shrilling laugh. He tripped and fell.
She picked him up before he turned to gold.
A game of tag with careless steps
all as her palace watched them run around.
Her palace watched them run around.
The phantom sunlight left its hive.
Yellow bristles giggled on her morning gown.
He let her catch him tons of times
all as her palace watched them run around.
Her palace watched them run around.

NEVERRIA. The reeds retain their gold because you
laugh.
The breeze divorced their courses back and forth
until your voice awoke to pave their path.
Their gusts will nurse the field your laugh explores.
Because they've never heard you all their life,
misunderstandments rot their point of view.
Your laughter lanas what they longed to like.
They'll never know or hear you like I do.
 Your laugh's permission grants an audience.
The reeds will never heckle nor will judge
as Love is shown to their applauding hands,
because these fields will never get enough.
FRANCO. So, let's perform their favorite scene again:
the scene where royal fingers meet my hand.

FRANCO. You sound so sure, unlike the nurse
who treats me like a straying dog.
But political slander blurs
because you tell me that she's wrong.
Assuring words, they leave your lips
to battle that revolution she'll start.
Oh, but I know we'll never lose
because the yellow reeds approve our Love.
The yellow reeds approve our Love.
Their summer dance, their waving hands;
the vast audience of bristles bow to us.
No one will stop our dazed romance
because the yellow reeds approve our Love.
NEVERRIA. The yellow reeds approve our Love.

NEVERRIA. The statue's clay returns to former dough.
I'll softly press and pull and knead your shape
until you're posed the way I want to hold;
a statue falling on my lap to lay.
Through paradise my fingers slowly row
to feel the strokes of paint which come alive;
a field of golden wheat without the crows
as clouds complain about their loss of time.
Ah, lucky hands so hold my renaissance
as fingers cup your chin and doughy cheeks
of which I'll pinch and play with when I want
because this art I see is art for me.
The way a hand will reach for paintings hung,
my fingers' steady row is never done.

FRANCO. The clouds I eyed have left the sky.
My neck no longer needs to crane.
My sanctuary's on your thighs,
where rests my head beneath your face.
Distracted fun, the skipping fluff;
they dragged me on their stroll and tugged my leash.
They'll never find my hiding spot.
Your beauty blocks the clouds I wished upon.
You block the clouds I wished upon.
They pass and stretch. Your silhouette.
You pet my hair like I'm some abandoned dog.
They skip away without their pet.
Your beauty blocks the clouds I wished upon.
You block the clouds I wished upon.

NEVERRIA. Camilla?

Is that this coming week's departure list?

CAMILLA. No, your highness. I am so sorry, Neverria.

FRANCO. What is it?

NEVERRIA. A letter of

impeachment? A summons to trial?

For what, Camilla?

CAMILLA. Love.

NEVERRIA. Oh. Tried for that.

Where did my shock become a ghost?

the time Geneva forced her toast.

To Franco.

CAMILLA. I'm sorry.

FRANCO. What has happened?

CAMILLA. Franco, wish! Your voice will stop this trial.

NEVERRIA. Geneva's heard him. All she did was groan.

CAMILLA. Oh. What will you do?

NEVERRIA. We'll stand the trial that Geneva's set

because we're proud about the Love we nurse.

We're both prepared to be found innocent

because we know this Love is not a curse.

CAMILLA. Fair Franco, juries ought to love your voice.

Pretend the judge is just a cloud

FRANCO. I'll tell the truth, and truly Love is true.

CAMILLA. And take the music out their memories

with words reviving roses that miss you.

Your voice will weed and vine their vanity.

NEVERRIA. You know a bit about his voice for what?

CAMILLA. I was his nurse.

NEVERRIA. I forgot.

Who hit his puppy-heart with scolding words

Who put him in the sad Narcissus Ward?

CAMILLA. No angel, Neverria.

I'll see you at tomorrow's trial.

NEVERRIA. Camilla? Will you testify for us?

CAMILLA. With frowning lips alert with hope I will.

My heart believes you both.

FRANCO. We'll win because our Love is law.

NEVERRIA. Yes, Franco.

At least Camilla's heart obeys the law.

I trust you most of all, Camilla, dear.

This loyalty is what the righteous sought

before corruption made the law unclear.

FRANCO. Thank you, Camilla.

CAMILLA. A week ago I watched your hands collide.

I'll never let your hands be pulled apart.

I watched them ride the air the garden sighed

where morning light was tanned to lull the dark.

Your glacier hands together met to chill.

If iced-hands melt, the Afterlove will flood.

Geneva would be paid a teary bill.

She'll see your frozen hands will not unlock.

NEVERRIA. Thank you, fair Camilla.

CAMILLA. Farewell.

UNSEEN ANGELS. A breeze proposed, the reeds declined
and pushed the breeze away to weep.
Juvenilely switching sides;
they rushed between the reeds and stream.
A broken splash, a giggled shout,
and up the yellow fields Camilla waved.
And up across the sandy fluff,
Their footprints stamped a sheet of music notes.
Their footprints stamped a sheet of notes.
"Come here, come here" it deeply cheered
as the grieving river begged them not to go.
Obliviously engineered;
their footprints stamped a sheet of music notes.
Their footprints stamped a sheet of notes.

UNSEEN ANGELS. Her eager grin, an honest crib.
She pat his head with tired sighs.
Electricity on her lips.
They zapped his smile back to life.
Below her neck, his hair was stretched
beneath her raven curtains ringed with gold.
She wiggled down beneath his weight
while he fell asleep inside her arms.
He fell asleep inside her arms.
Her arched elbows, his slouching throne,
with combing fingers that swatted away harm.
And smudged against her collar bone,
her Franco fell asleep inside her arms.
He fell asleep inside her arms.

UNSEEN ANGELS. The palace fields, its yellow quilt
witnessed him sink inside her hold.
Obediently staying still
they ogled at the couple's pose.
A summer warmth, the baking sun
with ceilings like a museum's walls of beige
where the couple's perfect sinking.
They laid. If only reeds were taught to sculpt.
If only reeds were taught to sculpt.
The lazy straw. They watched and awed
couples similar a statue's tired slump.
Renaissancilly daylight paused
to ask if only reeds were taught to sculpt.
If only reeds were taught to sculpt.

CAMILLA. An angel's lap has caught the artist's woes.
And like a hunter wooed to lay with swans,
he's still as nursing talons rake and comb.
She combs his hair where sorrow's not belonged.
A stadium of reeds spectate their game.
Perfectly pitched with poets up to bat.
Their huddled lips devise their winning play;
the pact of which no sorrow can combat.
He's safely falling in her harness arms.
Refrain from turning ivory feathers red
throughout their glide along their dotage dawn,
and crane your neck with mine as Love ascends.
Endangered breeds so hide inside the reeds.
Leave Franco in the palace. Leave them be.

GENEVA. Camilla, did you miss his manic toasts?
He loomed above the table in a trance
with shame stormclouds pretend to never hold.
It sobered what the mango wine had planned.
CAMILLA. She cups his face to rinse the sorrow out
as Neverria loathes how Franco hurt.
She's curing pain unlike the nurses' help.
GENEVA. She glamors in his tortured artist curse.
CAMILLA. I find his sadness beautiful and true.
GENEVA. It's true because it's rigored in his gaze.
This boy is not a leopard in a zoo,
despite the life he spent behind his cage.
Our queen has caught a fancy animal;
a thing to chain around her pinnacle.

CAMILLA. I heard a story that he can't forget.

GENEVA. His woe will wash away for paradise,
with zero sighs upon his spirits breath
if in the Heavens Franco's soul arrives.
I hope the queen will want her Franco healed
so that he can transcend to holy rest,
where he's not tangled in his failure's field;
the field the Heavens heal upon entrance.

CAMILLA. You think he failed? You think with life he
failed?

GENEVA. Enough to earn the title plenty times
His art is not behind the museum rails.
It's what has taught his tired soul to whine.

CAMILLA. Is Love so fun and popular to duel?
To hold its scruff inside your fist of rules?

GENEVA. And now you've lost the afternoon's debate.
I want this boy to heal and move along.
I'm heeding what an angel's honor says
alike your friend, Viola. Move along.
CAMILLA. I say the angels should admire art.
Perchance we swoop to search for what's ignored,
and art is what the mortal world forgot!
It's dusty; rarely valued anymore.
A queen admires Franco Finnegan.
She ogles like the scholar in the Louvre.
Her awe beholds her Franco's medicine,
and heals the mental pain he has been through.
GENEVA. Our queen's become a dark academic.
Her greed-excitement makes his pain a trend.

NEVERRIA. Where theaters swallow angels on their
break,

we'll watch a Lady Timon lose her wealth

because she lended all her gold to knaves;

a chance the greedy bards and jewelers pounce.

I still believe the play's a comedy.

A crater made of hula-hooping stairs!

the rich abandon all philosophy.

The souls of Athens truly never cared.

And when the play is done, we'll visit farms

where mangos ride the trees before they're mashed

the way I cling and hang against your arm.

FRANCO. And then we'll eat our dinner when we're
back?

NEVERRIA. Our favorite meals will mime welcome-home
signs;

a celebration in our palace light.

UNSEEN ANGELS. She tugged his hand. The tour began
where shingles slept as snug as grapes.
Directionlessly forward dance.
Her laughing lips hurrayed his name.
With stairs applauding racing steps,
the sunlight wept because it couldn't join.
With currents flirting at their clothes,
they pranced where villas wore damascus wine.
Where villas wore damascus wine.
She tugged his arm. He loved the pull.
Yellow patterns, scarlet roofs, and pillars white.
Intoxitory never dull,
they pranced where villas wore damascus wine.
Where villas wore damascus wine.

NEVERRIA. We wear tiaras made of olive leaves.
The morning light has rolled its carpet out,
and it appears the day'll frolic free.
Its touring shine unrolls to part the clouds
as all the pillars stand their stoic watch.
Our compass hearts command this random course
where solar blizzards sand the roads we cross;
a common part of touring grand resorts.
FRANCO. My guide's your pulling pair of eager hands
who teach the sun to reach and stretch its gold;
delighted fulls where summer meets the land.
I seek no other means to trek alone.
As sun is scraping night from every roof,
my Love is taking I with merry moves.

NEVERRIA. Your laughter's soap for marble stairs and
poles.
Without effort, you wake the ruins up.
And guiding, scrubbing, us! across their roads,
it's like the villas use me like their brush.
FRANCO. And Love will give society its bath.
The sun's a towel that detests its work.
We stop the dirt from haunting pebbled paths
as solar frowns are drying back and forth.
NEVERRIA. Our prints ferment between rebelling cracks,
for memory is such a drink for stone.
And when my palace takes its couple back,
we'll watch the villas try to stumble home.
FRANCO. Atop your balcony and in your arms?
NEVERRIA. Yes. After every bath is well and done.

NEVERRIA. No summer could remove your gothic glare.
The temples smooth their stone to rouse your eyes,
ah, but a ruder gloom is always there,
and tempts your viewing eyes to scout for night.
FRANCO. The shadows' sheets are asking where I went
throughout their crawl below where shoulders meet.
Their carols greet me like a former friend,
and, gullible, I hope they won't deceive.
NEVERRIA. We shoo their starless waves of black away.
We end their plea, and mute their yawning touch.
They swoop with cowardness. We sit unfazed.
You've been deceived and used beyond enough.
FRANCO. They cower when I sit beside my queen.
NEVERRIA. Because our time together's light to see.

NEVERRIA. As palace plants pretend to take their nap,
as limbo skies adore our picnic eyes,
my tired boy descends into my lap,
and lets me watch him look for lost July.
We've spun, and Babylon is waking up
with that forgotten color candles farm.
Upon these steps, I'll tell August to hush;
my icarus has landed in my arms.
Ah, everytime I plant my cleo kiss
and dive forward to peck upon your brow,
you blink to lock the euphoria in.
I'll kiss again if it ever gets out.
And such a fairytale is always here;
the gossip that our palace gardens share.

UNSEEN ANGELS. Their kitchen cave. His wishes baked,
and splotched with flour, couples laugh.
Confectionery wedding cakes,
they watched an angel grasp his back.
With bumping heads, their eyes reread
the menus on their slowly reaching lips.
As spoons suspent as still as bats,
alone, they stirred themselves around to dance.
They stirred themselves around to dance.
The flour's cloud. Their kneading mouths.
She stood inside his arms like another chance.
Respiratories sighing down.
Alone, they stirred themselves around to dance.
They stirred themselves around to dance.

FRANCO. And tell me what's the thing an angel bakes?
NEVERRIA. The answer often cools inside my arms;
the fellow that my bosom mantle takes.
FRANCO. No grander oven woos my eyes to drop.
NEVERRIA. These kitchen counters envy altars now
because your sweet responses cook the air,
and tricks the hours into falling down
as pots and pans rehearse a floral stare.
A steaming charm's embalmed behind your smirk.
Ah, cool upon my bedroom's window sill,
beneath the arch of pillars that are curved.
FRANCO. I'll never cool. Your warmth repels the chills.
NEVERRIA. So then with Love as hot as any sun,
our Love's eternal cooling's never done.

NEVERRIA. I'll teach my merry gothic how to bake.
Eternal honeymoons are in preheat
with scenes austerely tropical to taste
as gallows strobed with spoons pretend to sleep.
We give this lecture where reflections bloom.
Their silver petals sniff our fruity words;
the silver which our clear affections smooth
as glamor nestles in these spoons and forks.
FRANCO. You're like this kitchen's righteous dose of
Spring-
the breeze is in to wake its flowers up,
reviving wishes that the spoons have hid.
So teach me how you grace their rust to stop.
NEVERRIA. As every spoon reflects our current stance,
the major rule to bake is- take my hand.

NEVERRIA. Ah, let's embrace accusations for fun!
I'll lean and dangle on your shoulder's rind
as royal braids unscrew until unstrung
to sleep and cradle on your arm; my vine.
We'll make the court our orchard strewn with shock.
My angels been behaving like the crows,
so let a churchly organ shoo their flock.
As crows retreat, our fruit for wine will grow.
We're what the wedding organs talked about.
Its morgue of keys refrain a merry tune.
We'll act its grim and sweet essences out,
coercing juries that they sit in pews.
Displaying simple scenes of subtle Love,
we'll make the angels grieve deciding Law.

NEVERRIA. We need to dance as sunsets fall asleep.
The way a kid will watch a music box,
the sun will watch us on this balcony
as lullabies demand we never stop.
FRANCO. A dance to tire everybody out?
NEVERRIA. The clouds who watch. The stars who want
to watch
a music box's figures twirl around.
FRANCO. As villas doze below a sunset blush?
NEVERRIA. Yes. Take my hand and then I'll lead the
spin.
We'll twist before the villas' tanning surf
with subtle pauses, watching sunlight sink.
Night's told the morning that it should reverse.
The sunset wants a show. We can be that;
the reason that tomorrow's sun comes back.

UNSEEN ANGELS. Awaiting tea, and fighting sleep,
they sat with little things to think.
Exhaustionary in the suite
where daylight faded on their skin.
The clocks enjoyed this resting point
where wealthy eyes and solemn eyes equaled.
With timid bearing like a guard,
the patient servant watched the couple lounge.
The servant watched the couple lounge.
A cleo pause to rest their lungs,
slumping on each other on a velvet couch.
As pearly clouds patrolled and mopped,
the patient servant watched the couple lounge.
The servant watched the couple lounge.

NEVERRIA. Ah servant, sing a song to praise my boy,
and purr with mournful academic flair
to war the thinking gloss his gaze employs;
no torch compares to that authentic stare.
A voice to make the eye of Horus blink,
pretend to be a renaissancing flute,
and joy to make an idyll chorus sink.
Present a speech to mispronounce his gloom.
A sorrow's beauty sends him in a slump.
It weighs its treasure on his tired chest.
He burrows sweetly in my grimless arms;
a place he's better off and tired less.
So sing! Refrain from singing glad enough.
I wish his gaze to keep its saddened touch.

UNSEEN ANGELS. Archaic lines prolonged the sighs
an angel-servant had rehearsed.
As studiously lovers tried
to feel her wandering of words.
A pretty croon debated noon
as angel melody was scolding clouds.
A train of notes repolished gold
while an angel sang *Come Away Death.*
An angel sang *Come Away Death.*
The servant sang- content and soft,
haunted happily by Shakespeare's final breath.
A sweet harmony kept him goth
while an angel sang *Come Away Death.*
An angel sang *Come Away Death.*

ANGEL-SERVANT. My queen, your boy appears a bit
depressed.
I see a lazy sort of sadness shine.
His sweeter joy has steered to kiss regret.
FRANCO. I don't regret a thing. The fault's not mine.
NEVERRIA. His gift and pain's his artist harmony.
His talent's trailed by sorrow in his glare;
a fitting place to park his large defeat,
a malice brail he lets my fingers share.
It's rough no one has opened up his books.
His cheeks; my most beloved thing to pinch!
I love to cup his broke and sullen look,
and see him blink above my fingertips.
So look and see me read while I lay.
His face is ever on my favorite page.

FRANCO. Without concern, the temples burn
inside my mind where flames debate.
Respitingly, a song is served,
rewinding back to zenith days.
Beside my girl. Our ears are perked
as music matches phantoms' dusty speed
as singing ends, as sleep descends
to watch my ruined heart believe it's Rome.
My ruined heart believes it's Rome.
By music's sweat, my grief is swept.
Songs remove the veiny cracks along the stone.
Relaxing like I won a quest
because my ruined heart believes it's Rome.
My ruined heart believes it's Rome.

CAMILLA. The coven gathers in the palace court.
Their lips become a branch for perching doubt;
so heavy that their lips are slanting down.
Their every frown will fly to chase your words.
So, tell me, what you've penned inside your mind
and tell me what they'll chase this trial night.
What is your plan, Franco?
FRANCO. I'm just going to stand there.
CAMILLA. Stand there?
FRANCO. Well, Neverria's confident enough.
CAMILLA. You two devised a plan?
FRANCO. I guess.
CAMILLA. And, what's the plan?
FRANCO. To be ourselves.
CAMILLA. Amend this strife with sayings that astound!
I'm faithful in the words your lips invent.
Pretend they're like a lazy laying cloud.
They left their daily watch to hear you vent.

GENEVA. This Afterlove is not an underworld,
though Heaven's full of fairer sights eyevealed.
A pause between the life and death of souls;
where hurt romantic souls vacay to heal.
Here, Franco Finnegan excites our queen
who rules our grand rehab of broken hearts.
Her love excites herself as well as he
before his healing barely even starts.
Love's novel crown too vastly prayed about;
her head is tilting underneath its weight.
They lock their eyes til eyes are chained and bound.
She'll never see her kingdom's slanting state.
And angels, know her treason sin is this:
her Franco's kiss became our crucikiss.
He's standing stiff and stupid like a stooge.
And loosely swaying on his body's side,
her hands transmit lust through his ivory suit.
She slacks the further that her fingers drive.
Her fingers stir his chest to tend his pulse.
No chef constantly checks if pots are hot.
Their simmer curses guests inside their house;
forgetting everything except their Love.
NEVERRIA. And?
GENEVA. And?
NEVERRIA. What are you saying?

GENEVA. I'm saying that infatuation's drugged.
Your toxins course throughout asylum veins.
Oh, fangs misfire in the viper's blood-
this; like the venom which attacked the snake.
You stop the Afterlove from slithering
its path by making venom like a drink.
Now, that is my opening.
Neveria, what is your defense?
NEVERRIA. I love him.

NEVERRIA. Ah, Love is mad for finding spots to bud.
From places that the magma turned to tar,
to in my palace in the Afterlove;
it rises like a ribbon out from scars.
Is that a weed or daisy that is grown?
Forgive the one who pulls and yanks it out.
Too often people steal their petal-crowns
until nothing will grow upon the mulch.
I see a hundred seeds inside his eyes.
They guard his pupils in their pool of green.
They ease the thunder's sea inside the sky.
How they want to grow when he looks at me.
Though ex's make him shy and hesitant-
a crater still becomes the flower's crib.

FRANCO. My heart elects my knee's descent
as angels tell me what is true.
Conformatory like the rest
until I only kneel for you.
Oh, angels stop. I'll pick the heart,
and kneel until you pull me in a hug
as every angel watches us.
So let's be wed and dig debate its grave.
Let's wed and dig debate its grave.
My clasping palms. My prayer is done
when you see the sacred question in my gaze.
Will matrimony wet our lawn?
So let's be wed and dig debate its grave.
Let's wed and dig debate its grave.
NEVERRIA. The ground will catch my knee as well.
They could behead the both of us.
As "yes, I'll wed" becomes expelled
they'll hear the stars release their dust.

UNSEEN ANGELS. Their faces mashed. Geneva gasped.
Proposals used as last resorts?
She judgmentally grimaced at
the couple guilty on the court.
A pause for air where angels stared
and stayed silent amongst the awkward smacks.
With matrimony's guilty plea,
they made the gavel seek a wedding bell.
The gavel sought a wedding bell.
A trial kiss. A crucikiss.
It stole away the sound from out angel mouths.
Collisionary tidal lips;
it made the gavel seek a wedding bell.
The gavel sought a wedding bell.

GENEVA. Who lets empires interrupt themselves?
I've never seen a girl with power kneel.
Their knees descend and sink for something else.
Oh, but how does the ground of limestone feel?
I lash my eyes away from failure's whip.
They kneel; I feel I'm lying on my chest
with failure's whip demanding that I squint.
Its crack adores them, but mutes mine protest.
I've seen the aftermath of men's work.
Perhaps my mind is clogged with bleak prequels;
my patients sobbing in the corridors.
And now she kneels as if he's her equal?
Who lets empires interrupt themselves?
Their knees descend and sink for something else.

VIOLA. I left. Camilla's crying tears of joy.

GENEVA. Why don't we weep for weddings like she weeps?

CAMILLA. With Love, you let yourselves remain annoyed.
Verdunned, trespassing in its phantom scenes
where broken hearted people slouch and mourn
the Love they thought they'd never lose before.

VIOLA. Camilla, that's our duty in this world.

CAMILLA. If fallen knees present this world me tears,
I think we should present the ground our knees
and clasp our palms and pray with mournful cheer,
worshiping what will make an angel weep.

GENEVA. My face has not tattooed itself with tears.
No crystal streams migrate along my cheeks.
They stay padlocked aloof to dwell elsewhere.
No special scene will let my tears release.
Enough. This talk about our tears' absurd.
I don't desire speaking anymore.

CAMILLA. The queen bestowed upon me a request.
The maid of honor! That's the thing she asked.
She knows their Love so stirs and brews my breath.
The maid of honor.
Oh, great sonatas splash my bridesmaid sash.
Pachelbel and pianos. The songs the churches love.

Hm, Viola? What do you think about that, honorable
Viola?

GENEVA. An angel wedding? What a thought to scoff.
And mortals often think we're wedding guests.
They'd find themselves surprised to know our job.
It's all them that destroy and make their best.

.

NEVERRIA. Geneva, slumped upon the stairs for what?

GENEVA. Defeat's a heavy pair of epaulets.

NEVERRIA. I'd guess you're waiting on a rascal thought?

GENEVA. Oh, stop. My rascal thought's engaged I guess.

NEVERRIA. Ah, serve your rascal thoughts with loosened grip,

and make your house of thought an anarchy.

The free'est throne is where brilliance sits.

To stop a rascal thought's a tragedy.

GENEVA. I've been attempting what I think is best.

The rascal's won his stooge rebellion,

and now my throne is just these thoughtless steps.

Fiascos dawn above where halos sit.

NEVERRIA. Embrace fiascos in the time of Love.

GENEVA. You do so every night when day is done.

NEVERRIA. Geneva! Be another bridal maid.

Rejoice instead of skulking in defeat

Who knows. Perhaps you'll catch the rogue bouquet.

Be something that defeat will so envy.

GENEVA. How could you offer such a sudden truce?

The thing I tried to choke with gavel hands.

NEVERRIA. Distrust is not welcome inside our group.

CAMILLA. Geneva! Yes! Together let us stand.

GENEVA. It all depends upon the color dress.

NEVERRIA. I'm gonna make my wedding gown a pink.

It's not my Franco's favorite color yet.

Ah, but it should be when I'm done with him.

CAMILLA. Geneva's shoulders need a yellow strap.

NEVERRIA. So, wear the shades April desires back.

CAMILLA. This plagued my heart already in a fritz.

NEVERRIA. Of what domain?

CAMILLA. Happiness.

GENEVA. An angel on the better side of Love?
My queen invites me on the wedding barge.
Perhaps I should obey their hearts' applause,
and shun the law dictating Afterlove.
Their paradise intrudes my duty's norm;
a norm my queen no longer comprehends.
Her pair of eyes remove his inner storm?
Perhaps they mute the hurting that he's fled.
The duty angels serve? Or serve my queen?
I'll dive with bridal gowns prepared to soak
as uniforms will burn with smoke I breathe.
The flame of self-betrayal is not as cold.
An angel on the better side of Love.
I know I should obey their hearts' applause.

GENEVA. Oh, Neverria what a dress you don.

How eyes will bake with wanting at your dress.

It's stolen pink from jealous macarons,

and glides a pace of haunting wonderlust.

NEVERRIA. And what about Camilla's curtain peel?

The tropics want their timid ore returned.

She wears the thing the villas sit to feel;

a solar color that the reeds allured.

CAMILLA. Geneva's in the same ethereal silk,

with runes perfectly ruffled down her waist.

A neater grin the sun has yet to spill.

It noons against Geneva's form today.

NEVERRIA. Here, triple pillars stand with springly gowns,

here, wearing what's the brightest shade around.

GENEVA. I'm shocked to say I find myself intrigued.

It tightens on me everytime I spin

before this mirror where our stance repeats,

and loosens, hoping that I spin again.

NEVERRIA. And when my wedding ends, prepare to twirl

before we even savor any wine.

Your healthy stupor's in the mirror's girl.

Adore her. Drink reflections every night.

Ah, let the halls adopt a rich allure,

appearing like a nineteen-twenties club.

And speck the walls with candles' sparkled purs,

oranging night with candles' flirty touch.

So stupefy yourself with beauty's spell,

and fit the after-parties weddings dwell.

CAMILLA. So, bridesmaids gather on this balcony-
Oh, wait, has Franco picked his groomsmen yet?
NEVERRIA. No men bestow availability.

Giggles.

They're all constrained inside asylum vests.
GENEVA. And where is Franco at the moment now?
NEVERRIA. He went to walk throughout the reeds to
think.
I think he's practicing a gloomy bow
because an artist thought has struck him.
GENEVA. Perhaps he's out there searching for
groomsmen.
CAMILLA. And did he ask if groomsmen would attend?
NEVERRIA. I read his novel glare this afternoon
and only read his suite of passion's tomb.
encompassed in the Love he has for me;
no longer sad, and not as sorry.
CAMILLA. Perhaps we'll end this afternoon with tea?
NEVERRIA. I think that's fitting, Camilla.
GENEVA. You two go on without me.
I'm gonna take my time to awe myself one more time.

NEVERRIA. We'll make you a cup when you're ready,
Geneva.

GENEVA. The glass has caught my figurine's tattoo,
and makes me feel as Venus in the sea.
Geneva, in the mirror, is that you?
or are appeasements teasing what I see?
A mirror's never been this much polite.
Is glass distorting what I really am?
as alien reflections touch my sight.
Or's beauty what my sight has rarely scanned?
Reflections curse with sacred want to gaze.
The glass's rainbow stain has turned to blonde;
a lemon curtain praying down my waist.
This happy angel waned her burdens gone.
Their marriage breaks the rules I vow to keep.
Their nearing day; a smooch I'm proud to see.

FRANCO. Beyond the grave, my pain remains
until somebody reads my books.
Expediously marriage came,
and veils the final sigh I took.
Perhaps I'm meant to always mourn.
Are artists forced to sigh eternal sighs
despite the final vow of Death?
Are all the Afterlife's this bittersweet?
Are all the Afterlife's this sweet?
An angel's Love. My crusted brush,
dry and like my novels that they'll never read.
Ah! Matrimony's wealthy calm.
Are all the Afterlife's this bittersweet?
Are all the Afterlife's this sweet?

UNSEEN ANGELS. Confessional; the booth was full.
She pulled him in before he passed.
Ragamuffiny stubborn wool;
his hair for her fingers to pat.
His boutonniere again appeared,
lopsided on his chest before she helped,
and smoothed the wrinkles on his suit.
Camilla licked her palm to comb his hair.
She licked her palm to comb his hair.
She double-checked. Concerning gaze.
His hair laid again, pretending not to care.
She studiously pinched his face.
Camilla licked her palm to comb his hair.
She licked her palm to comb his hair.

UNSEEN ANGELS. By angel nails, the lutes exhaled,
as scents of wine hygened the air.
Celebratory laughter sailed
throughout the crowded palace stairs.
The jealous sky censored daylight,
and up there daunting strokes of gray patrolled.
The party's flood; it hushed the dark
as subtle music roused a renaissance.
The music roused a renaissance.
Between their chats, the angels laughed
above the fairytales the violins brought.
And plucking strings were laughing back
as subtle music roused a renaissance.
The music roused a renaissance.

NEVERRIA. My wolfish boy who taught my heart to
nurse;
he spent his hours drawn to rogue pursuits.
A wolf anoints itself with warmer fur,
unlike he that adons this ivory suit.
He taught himself a canine discipline,
to find the thing he longed for on his own.
Ah, but he dwelled his days with thinner skin
despite the winter Law upon Man's world.
My arms so warm this rogue and wounded wolf
who shivered in his passion that they shunned.
His charm disarmed the throne and wooed my soul.
He lives here in a fashion that they want!
And now he's warm enough to safely melt
because my arms' become my Franco's pelt.

NEVERRIA. Below this balcony our party stirs
the way the hurricanes pretend to waltz.
They glow with royalty's so-shiny blur,
and say and hush our names to venue walls.
This after party's foamed with cushioned bliss.
Geneva even swarms with bridal maids!
FRANCO. Because your happy tone is lush to sip.
It weaved this evening warmth an idyll fame.
NEVERRIA. Ah, hear the flutes of wine obey the toast?
FRANCO. I see them raise their drink alike a torch.
They spear their juice to strike the nighttime's coal;
beneath the night where mobs have changed their course.
NEVERRIA. We've marveled long enough above our guests.
I think they want to see the newlyweds.

NEVERRIA. You party like a caesar on their knees,
and stand with praying eyes who ask to kneel.
The heart I like has seized my monarchy!
demand your gaze to rise and catch this zeal.
The angels throw this triumph in our fame.
If joy is not discovered in their crowd,
my hands'll help you find it in my gaze-
my joining palms will cup your chin to crown.
Tonight is not a broken chariot.
You're used to crashing on utopic roads,
and sliding off the paths a leader sets.
Don't view it back as venues strobe with gold.
Tonight's the night to rise upon the stairs.
It's not the night for eyes to practice glare.

GENEVA. You know, a strange belonging haunts their
dance.
She fuels the smile that refuels the crowd,
and throws her smile-armored king again.
CAMILLA. It's funny that he's yet to stumble down.
GENEVA. Always returning like a boomerang,
she catches Franco in a pause of laughs,
before she gives the crowd her king again
before angel laughter sends him back.
CAMILLA. They choreograph with connecting eyes.
Nobody could repeat their orbit's route
as merry music masks my breathy sigh,
a thousand other muffled ones are felt.
GENEVA. The crowd of lungs surround the busy heart;
so sigh as dancing couples beat their job.

VIOLA. My gosh! He looks prepared to chase the moon.
How many cups of wine has Franco had?
GENEVA. Eh, not enough to wisen any stooge.
CAMILLA. Enough to keep a stooge's wife unmad.
I think the kiss has made him drunk tonight.
GENEVA. I saw he had his third a bit ago.
VIOLA. Perhaps to muffle something on his mind.
CAMILLA. Ha! Not with Franco's wife so beautiful.
A happy heart defeats the shout of thought.
VIOLA. His thoughtful shout is hard to beat and mute,
returning when alcohol's wearing off.
CAMILLA. Well, call me wine because you should go
shoo.
GENEVA. Her Franco's being merry, not a drunk.
He would've puked by now with how he's spun.

UNSEEN ANGELS. With locking eyes, he took her sides
as lutes were thrilled to scratch the air.
Choreography on the fly,
they swayed with what the torches shared.
As angels filled the palace hall,
the wine perfumed the sweetest wedding speech.
Her awing look. His hundredth blink.
As angels danced the purgatory bop
they danced the purgatory bop.
With bowing heads, he watched her smirk,
and the feel of being like a zombie stopped.
Reassuringly looks were words.
As angels danced the purgatory bop
they danced the purgatory bop.

NEVERRIA. Isn't my drunk and dancing husband cute?

He wishes that we offered beer instead.

GENEVA. I think you're smitting over such a stooge.

NEVERRIA. My stooge! I understand his muddled head.

CAMILLA. My goodness. Watch the angels cheer him on.

This hall has never seen a jolly jig,

and now it watches Franco nearly fall;

a sip away from thinking that he sings.

NEVERRIA. I'm lucky that I'll haul him off to sleep.

I love assisting Franco everywhere.

Us laying; that is when the night's complete.

GENEVA. Your mind, my queen, how much wine is in there?

NEVERRIA. The wine of words his eyes release for Love.

Excuse me but I need another gulp.

NEVERRIA. Ah, angels all behold my moody boy.
He's drugged with talent- sober in my hug.
A plain and awful mold he did avoid
because he picked his art and not a job.
Pianos said they're sorry when he laughed,
until they played the notes they're told to play.
And tidal waves reversed to pave his path.
Oh, but no state condones the prints he made.
The misers need their minions in the mill,
and art requires dreamers in their room.
With Life besieged by Men demanding bills,
the artists die beneath the misers rule.
Without an ounce of greed, I love my king,
my novel king, my Franco Finnegan.

UNSEEN ANGELS. As kisses popped, he sobered up
and standing still her kisses hit.
Her sovereignty of fingers cupped
to hold the cheeks she loved to pinch.
A thankful queen. Her wanting eyes.
He lost the need to mute his thoughts with wine.
Her lips reminded Franco that
before the angels watched her lead him out.
The angels watched her lead him out.
From out the hall, and up the stairs
the married skipped with a trick-or-treating bout.
Their fingers curled. She gripped with care,
ignoring angels as she led him out.
The angels watched her lead him out.

NEVERRIA. We make the rings of saturn envious
throughout this carousel of bouncing twirls.
Our chaining fingers pack the weightlessness
from space where stars will swell to mock the pearls.
FRANCO. The pillows fling to mock the comets' course!
NEVERRIA. Because our zestful orbit whips them out.
With thrill, we spin. We jump. We summon more
as all our restless urges spin around.
FRANCO. We're like our bed's appointed satellite,
although my eyes become distracted now.
NEVERRIA. Your eyes are sending singles that I like.
They throne and dive throughout this mattress bounce.
As further wanting in your eyes appears-
ah, cute enough to cure a mona leer.

NEVERRIA. Ah, husband, hold me in this lunar flood.
Tonight there's hints of sugar in the stars
because they glow and wink to view your blush.
I like the thing they put here in my arms.
FRANCO. I'd crane my neck inside a forest sigh
to shroud my breath with songs the cosmos sang.
I'd gaze its heavens when I was alive,
and now my neck no longer needs to crane.
My galaxy commands and guides my eyes.
Your arm's the belt of stars I now obey
with orreries of fingers that's my guide.
It charms myself to wander where you say.
NEVERRIA. Your wondered eyes became my favorite
ship.
To steer- my gentle fingers hold your chin.

NEVERRIA. Your eyes are weighed with sweet
exhaustion's plague.
I see they're packed to travel into sleep,
so lie and lay to ease your gothic pain.
These sheets'll catch the battle that you grieve.
FRANCO. Forbid my eyes to fall unless alove.
They close so easily below your mouth
with which you sigh a fall of breathless thoughts,
so close to sweetening this nightly drowse.
NEVERRIA. My arm's a cradle that'll hold your neck.
My ears already hold your every word.
"An angel's wrist." How could I forget?
It clears the frenzy storms attempt to storm.
FRANCO. And now these angel wrists arrest my soul.
NEVERRIA. They proudly grant your wish, my dear
Franco.

UNSEEN ANGELS. The night refilled its inky spill
as ends to wedding nights began.
Apprehensively standing still,
afraid and shy to raise his hand.
With queens asleep, he sulked and sneaked
throughout the halls as every angel slept.
With beautifully somber pace
he pictured that his paintings draped the walls.
If only paintings draped the walls.
The hieroglyphs, their opal ink,
forbidding any paintings be shown at all.
A visionary cursed to wish;
he pictured that his paintings draped the walls.
If only paintings draped the walls.

GENEVA. The party's even tired out the ghosts,
and leisured dusk admires royal grooms,
with darkness leading tired angels home.
CAMILLA. Geneva, hush! Is that the boy we knew?
Asylum gardens memorized this boy.
He gossips in a language that is mute
with eyes disarming wedding nights their joy.
His chronic sting of damage never cooled.
GENEVA. He should be busy on his wedding night
instead of staring at the palace walls.
And what's so urgent that he left his wife?
Her bed is barren while husbands walk.
CAMILLA. He still is grieving starry starry nights.
Too ill to weep. Oh, sorry sorry sight.

FRANCO. Imagine that my paintings plate this wall.
They'd fill the eye with sad and subtle pride.
I guess my tragic gaze explains it all;
I'd still be writing had their eyeballs tried.
GENEVA. Imagine that your wife is waking up
to find her husband on a zombie walk.
FRANCO. I haven't passed a night without this rut,
and nightly must my melancholy stalk.
CAMILLA. You come here every night to dream and wish?
FRANCO. I pace the palace when she falls asleep,
for dusk is happy when I'm insomnic.
CAMILLA. She'd hate your absence. Go return and dream.
FRANCO. Oh nurse, I think to wish is now to mourn.
I'll go because my wishes plow no more.

UNSEEN ANGELS. A palace tour with irked escorts;
his arms became their shoulders' scarfs.
Choreography like a corpse;
exhausted after mourning art.
As moonlight fell, he weighed them down.
He knew a ghost was meant to walk alone.
Geneva missed the gurney's help
as angels walked the artist back to bed.
The angels walked him back to bed.
The torches napped- pajamas black.
In between the angels, Franco bowed his head.
The three avoided eye contact
as angels walked the artist back to bed.
The angels walked him back to bed.

CAMILLA. Eternal dreams descend eternal falls
inside a never-ending wishing well.
This limbo seems to end no fall at all.
Instead of pennies, Franco threw himself.
There's coins who beg for help between his blinks.
They'll never meet the tears they want to splash.
Oh, that expression scares the hieroglyphs
as coins are things no fountains ever catch.
The air constantly cuts itself with coins
wherever Franco aims his wish at clouds.
They put a ceiling up above the boy,
and now Forever's never coming down.
Was wishing worth his mother's cries of pain?
She can't behold his wishful eyes today.

CAMILLA. I think this palace needs a library;
a vague reminder that'll lull your spouse.
To sink the malice that's his tragedy,
and tame his mind between a hall of shelves!
NEVERRIA. A wedding gift for Franco Finnegan?
CAMILLA. A garden full of books he read and wrote.
And like an orphanage for canvases,
the second floor will let his paintings roam.
NEVERRIA. His very own elusive gallery;
a gala full of novels that distract.
CAMILLA. And books perhaps will treat his tragedy.
NEVERRIA. There's still a tragedy inside him packed?
CAMILLA. His literature is begging not to rust,
so let a church for art be risen up.
NEVERRIA. He's sleeping. Fetch Geneva.
Ah, plans have never loved me like this much before.

GENEVA. There's giddy squeals awaiting in your eyes.

NEVERRIA. Excitement's breeze delivers new ideas!

GENEVA. So, give me signs and hints of what's devised.

CAMILLA. Delight will leap and wink its lunar glare!
For Franco's pain to deadly less and less,
we'll raise a study that he can adopt.

NEVERRIA. His thankful gaze already bests my breath.

CAMILLA. The day the study's done- his pain will stop.

GENEVA. You'll build a study where he can relax?

NEVERRIA. Throughout construction, hide him in the ward,
and when it's done- you'll bring my Franco back
to paradise unlike it was before.
I'll visit every single night and day
until his study's shingles cry his name.

NEVERRIA. I've heard my Franco crying in his sleep;
a sound the birds of night revere to hear.
They learn from chants of whining; timid, sweet.
I've found their words have dived to dreary cheers.
Confused about why herons' gone away,
he wakes with looks my fingers reassure;
removing doubts appearing on his face.
I say, there'll never ring a sweeter curse.
Though fingers on his face comfort and ease,
I want his woe to whine and fly elsewhere
Ah, bring an honest place to thwart his grief,
where pages flip; the light delights to hear.
If libraries for Franco build and rise,
they'll banish all the tears I've heard him cry.

UNSEEN ANGELS. Before he woke, the angels rushed
and stole him like they did before.
Reunionary gardens blushed
as gurneys rolled between the ferns.

GENEVA. A puppy's in today's Narcissus Ward,
though not a bark has sought a friend or treat.
He's truly in a daze of missing her.
He's stopped himself with trauma's trend of grief.
VIOLA. And now we'll heal the bite his ex had left.
GENEVA. Viola, Love has done our job for us!
Their vows have healed the crimes of Franco's ex.
I hope a lot is done, and quick enough.
I hate this sudden library idea.
We've stole a dove who longed for freedom's touch,
and name this punishment a sweet affair.
VIOLA. We roam this realm to do that as such.
GENEVA. This made me wishy washy, can't you tell?
VIOLA. I- for now, let's do our jobs. Do them well.

UNSEEN ANGELS. The angels spoke assuring tones
because they knew about the plan.
Therapeutically garden strolls-
the poet searched the shrubs for hands.
They brought him tea and books to read
and watched him in the cafeteria.
Distractionary clinic stay
as all the angels never left his side.
The angels never left his side.
They walked their pet; their special guest.
Franco's lips forgot the taste of mango wine.
He failed his shemp escape attempts
because the angels never left his side.
The angels never left his side.

GENEVA. Your slouch has made your shoulders like
they're slides.
And sorrow's children ride it down your back,
with giggles that attract the summertime.
Their stomping must annoy the playground's grass.
Here. Never strive to prove your tragedy.
You left your novels, which will not depart.
Survive inside a student memory,
and let tomorrow's children find your art.
FRANCO. Without a queen to hug, it floods my mind.
She casted out my grief- my exorcist.
GENEVA. Oh, doubt this grief. You left your touch
behind.
Though dead, your books and paintings still exist.
FRANCO. Who read them but the angel that I wed?
I miss her poems of lips upon foreheads.

FRANCO. Is simple good? It's left me shook
as instapoets publish shit.
Popularity's selling books.
Their lack of meter makes me sick.
Is Atticus *that* brilliant
as Rupi Kaur destroys her enter key?
They type
alike,
and kill
this art.
Somebody tell me art is still alive!
Who'll tell me art is still alive?
They write cliches. The pages waste
because they only use a page for three lines.
Will Edgar Allan Poe awake
to shake and tell me art is still alive?
Who'll tell me art is still alive?

UNSEEN ANGELS. With moping done, he turned to run
before the angels pushed him down.
An angel posse huddled up
atop him on the garden's ground.
Beneath their words, he rolled and squirmed,
aggravated about an artist's weight
which sent him rolling back and forth
to fit below a limbo summer sky.
Below a limbo summer sky.
Against the stone, they pinned his wrists,
and held him better as he tried not to cry.
Franco winced,
so lost below a limbo summer sky.
Below a limbo summer sky.

NEVERRIA. This half constructed study's like a wreck
where sirens like me seek their Icarus.
My saddened husband truly flied the best,
though tides were paid beneath his dripping wrists.
This roofless room rebuked by morning's rule
with pillars tricked to think they're naked masts.
This room refuses moving- like a tomb.
These starving bookshelves want their zombies back.
His absence matched with morning light is weird,
and makes this grungy room a haunted beach.
It packs my rap with tortured whine to hear;
mermaids forgot to let their hostage breathe.
Is all this worth the end result's surprise?
Asylums swallow men, and then their wives.

NEVERRIA. His hand increases weight if not with mine,
so heavy in awaiting mellow songs.
Remember when I held it in the night?
beneath the canopy of black applause.
Our feather fingers hovered on our breath
between the laughs throughout our dance to jazz.
And now these feathers faster fall to depth,
becoming tired on my palm's compass.
As seagulls yawn throughout their lazy trip
my hand's extended in his voice's lack;
about to drop inside a cold abyss.
Exhausted wings so wish he could come back.
So, Franco, let my tired fingers land,
and skid and scrape to safety on your hand.

GENEVA. As night enjoyed its wasted tar of light,

we chased him down the hall the nurses track.

Asylum foyers- gates to paradise.

I pinned him down, and angels turned him back.

NEVERRIA. He needs a smoothing that's from harvest palms,

to lead his gaze away from checkered floors,

to see his muse is back to war this wrong.

This scheme I've made has made us wrecked and bored.

GENEVA. Construction's set to finish in the month.

Imagine what surprise his eyes will beam!

NEVERRIA. Construction's set a spirit free to haunt!

a tragic haunt's alive inside this week.

Ah, loneliness has never been this loud.

This study needs a better faster sprout.

NEVERRIA. My chin is not alike my Franco's chin.
My palm and fingers long his chin instead
as morning on my balcony begins
where fingers long to make his face caressed.
My wounded wolf who taught my heart to howl!
Awake and wave away the lamest stage
which morning boasts above the tired owl.
Awake and hoot a murmur of my name.
Before the yellow reeds welcome the sun,
he'll pry himself from bed where sunlight fasts.
Before the fountains whisper "night is done"
we'll try and hear the water's diamond scratch.
This palm'll pull him out from morning sleep,
and put his eyes upon the path to me.

FRANCO. My fingers dig the garden's kale
to search for fingers held before.
Desiratory fingers sail,
but they find themselves pricked by thorns.
They prick my hand. A scolding branch
where ivy needles bite my hand away
so that my hand is weeded out.
Oh, how the thorns remind me that she's gone.
The thorns remind me that she's gone.
A sorry stream. My knuckles bleed
as the hedges teach me not to reach for Love.
Rejectionary pricking leaf.
Oh, how the thorns remind me that she's gone.
The thorns remind me that she's gone.

CAMILLA. Help! Geneva! Franco's hands are bleeding!
Give me anything to stop the bleeding!
The fingers that made the canvas sweetened;
growing limp and pale because they're bleeding!
Fingers searched the green for what he needed;
his queen. Without her his hands are bleeding!
Help me mute his knuckles' scarlet speeches!
Help! Geneva! Franco's hands are bleeding!
Tell the roses not to start their grieving!
Tell the leaves to look away. He's bleeding!

CAMILLA. Without a wish, we get the gift
and sprouting swift we lose its sight.
Ethereally caught with ink
because it passed the artist's eye.
A painter's tear, a healing brush.
Pianist fingers jump from key to key,
and Darwinary theories fade
because the artist's fingers look for God.
The artist's fingers look for God.
He graced his most unworthy hands
so his poetry will never get to stop,
for when he hurt, he wrote again
because the artist's fingers look for God.
The artist's fingers look for God.

GENEVA. I think- I think there's been an accident,
for gardens never lose their weight so fast
as light retreats to find where magic went,
as darkness lingers, light attempts to track.
Camilla? Crying? In this garden's court?
I'll follow what your voice retrieves and gives;
a spill of crying that you bark so hoarse.
CAMILLA. Her Franco caught the thorns. They cleaved
his wrists!
GENEVA. Camilla- wait- you're covered in his blood.
CAMILLA. I tried to stop the bleeding out his arms.
I pressed, and pressed and pressed oh not enough!
GENEVA. Camilla, come here. Now it's-
CAMILLA. We just ignored his raw soliloquies!
because of that... the tortured artist bleeds.

CAMILLA. I come with news, the gravest news.

Inside the garden's maze he died.

Catatonicly missing you,

he searched the thorns to find his wife.

NEVERRIA. Ah! Stop your tongue! Ah! Stop your

tongue!

I want him back before you speak again!

This prank disgusts me, Camilla.

This library's almost complete and done,

so bring him back to see it now.

CAMILLA. I'm so sorry, Neverria.

God has signed his name on the departure list,

and now our Franco's in His care.

The thorns replayed the past upon his wrists.

The thorns have- the thorns have-

Cries.

NEVERRIA. A poet only heard by angel ears!
The crooked cane has raked him into Death!
CAMILLA. He's floated only toward the Heavens' piers,
and art survives as sacred evidence.
NEVERRIA. My merry gothic's gone-
CAMILLA. His artist prints remain to never fade
unlike the blood my apron's forced to wear,
and all it takes is eyes upon a page.
NEVERRIA. His blood is sprinkled on your uniform;
the dots and streaks of scarlet cursive's whip!
Was that how blood was splattered on the earth?
CAMILLA. Sha-shake your head with me, and just don't
think.
And all it takes is eyes upon a page.
NEVERRIA. Camilla. Go away. Camilla. Stray.

NEVERRIA. Where novels dwell, this sunlight swells
and shelves pretend he never left.
Has purgatory pleased itself?
by letting artists bleed to death.
A roofless room- it's incomplete.
Libraries envy Roderick Usher's house,
and wedding bells pretend they're hooves.
This study's desk becomes the altar stone.
This desk becomes the altar stone.
A life of art. His broken heart!
and where's his never noticed sacrifice throned?
The praying sun performs its part.
This study's desk becomes the altar stone.
This desk becomes the altar stone.

NEVERRIA. Cleopatra lived inside the Widow Ward.
She scampered in the aisles donning dust,
for Marc Antony fell upon his sword
before the viper turned her gold to rust.
I'll rip these curtains, break the vase and screech
where shattered glass apologies lie
with broken pieces stretched below my reach
throughout my reach for artists not alive.
Perhaps I'm really like her after all.
Ah, but she did adore a warrior.
My catch was built to let the wars be stalled.
We ruined both. I ruined mine more. More!
With pens and brushes gone, the vipers rule
and sets an angel's insanity loose.

NEVERRIA. I want him back. I want my asp.
No servant could retrieve the two.
Unfinished studies stay unpacked
where novels wait to wake. They're fools.
The party's stopped. My trophy's dropped
because its handles scratched a wall of thorns.
It can't be stood upon these shelves
where flakes of dust attempt to mime our twirl.
The dust attempts to mime our twirl.
He would've liked this morning light
rejected light who wanted to work for pearls.
And enviously royal eyes
are watching dust attempt to mime our twirl.
The dust attempts to mime our twirl.

NEVERRIA. A wooden lawn where dust is drawn;
the bookshelves seem to call his name.
Immortality's reading wrong.
Without him here, I feel my age.
This library's a mausoleum.
Tombstones and novels want their titles read
as canvases are staying still.
Pretend they're cemetery statuettes.
They're cemetery statuettes.
These naive shelves. A Mary's pout,
reaching out for phantoms that they'll never get.
You stupid shelves! You never helped!
Pretend you're cemetery statuettes.
You're cemetery statuettes.

UNSEEN ANGELS. With lifting arms, she put it on;
a golden headband on her brow.
Ornamentary diamonds yawned
to stop her wit from falling down.
Below her hair, above her eyes
with tassels like the feathers on a swan.
Reflections tried to compliment
as all her Isis style lost the world.
Her Isis style lost the world.
With scarab shade, her portrait gaze
wondered why she pouted while wearing gold.
Unconfidently resting face
as all her Isis style lost the world.
Her Isis style lost the world.

NEVERRIA. Will readers dance ballet inside his tomb,
or not because he wouldn't choose a job?
Will teachers plant his name inside classrooms?
I want to watch this haunted music box!
Where went the gallop flight of reading eyes?
with thoughtful lashes whipping heartbeat hooves.
Protecting ballad rhymes from reapers' scythes,
they crossed the paths of cryptic pencils' routes.
If people plant their eyes upon his words,
and let the roots of feeling break a mulch,
the easel's stance will thrive so undisturbed-
ah, let them view the spiels his aching sprouts.
Alas, he can't promote his art again.
They pass their hand with "no", and darkness wins.

UNSEEN ANGELS. Her vesper stance, extending hands
and dressed with pink she led a prayer.
Memorboricly in a trance;
she never let a tear appear.
As angel nurses wore their white,
staring down the closed and empty casket,
her bubblegum attire popped.
She wore her pinkest gown to mourn her boy.
And wearing pink she mourned her boy.
A sithic pause. Her train of thought
missed the glint of cursive that his hand employed.
To truly wonder what was lost,
why wear her pinkest gown to mourn her boy?
And wearing pink she mourned her boy.

VIOLA. With looks of caring seldom on her face,
our hostess throws a noir funeral.
She looks prepared to welcome in the Fates
amongst the clouds a mourner wooes to fall.
CAMILLA. Yes. Fog is crawling on the roads today.
I think it's Franco's wishes falling down
to sloth about and find a home to stay.
VIOLA. Here just to ask the queen to wander out.
GENEVA. You're lucky that your whispers spare her ears
throughout her watch before the casket's door
as thoughtful eyes await the disappeared
as waves of fog are snaking on the floor.
CAMILLA. The ghosts of wedding parties crawl as well
to toast this dreadful grayness that rebels.

CAMILLA. I saw her in her room before the dawn.

She stood before her mirror's backwards bow.

I watched her put her golden headband on;

a saturn belt above exhausted brows.

I think I sounded timid when I spoke.

She wrapped her raven hair with rosy shawls

ignoring what I asked a breath ago;

a gypsy busy with her crystal ball.

GENEVA. You make her lack of words so magical.

VIOLA. A cosmic pause is what her Franco did

the days we had him in our hospital.

CAMILLA. And now her eyes are miming silent hymns.

With not a word to say, we hear it all

by watching how her comet gazes fall.

UNSEEN ANGELS. A meek parade, their slothing pace
across a bridge the palace stretched.
A sarcophagus led the way
as angels moped behind its trek.
Towards other ends where bridges end,
where palace tombs revealed its yawning,
it ominously smoothly sailed.
They trailed the casket floating down the bridge.
The casket floated down the bridge.
The queen was walking in the front
as beneath the bridge the villas paled their tints.
A gallowary salem walk,
they trailed the casket floating down the bridge.
The casket floated down the bridge.

GENEVA. The fog has formed the tomb's accretion disk.
I feel it on my ankles; cool and damp,
requesting that the angels join its ring
as Franco's casket heeds the cobwebs' chant.
VIOLA. The palace tomb unwraps a humming sound,
almost releasing gusts against our queen.
The casket's drifting ever closer now.
I fear she'll try and chase it in her grief.
CAMILLA. His wishes worked and now the clouds
descend.
Too late they all agreed to grant his wish,
and now they swirl and form this saturn bend.
The perfect modern artist's posthumous.
GENEVA. The tomb's consumed the casket finally,
and thankfully our queen has yet to flee.

CAMILLA. No longer lives. His casket's sailed
and leaves our queen upon the bridge.
Illusionary hope has failed,
and stole a second chance to kiss.
Asylum noons, my eagle view,
I watched and spied upon the balcony
as Franco moped and held the rose.
I heard his soliloquies beg for Love.
His soliloquies begged for Love.
This morning chill, the queen is still
wondering if Franco ever got enough.
Are soliloquies unfulfilled?
She knows his soliloquies begged for Love.
His soliloquies begged for Love.

CAMILLA. Our counterparts have wandered back to work

and left our angel trio on the bridge

as sound departs from ponds of fog explored.

VIOLA. A tremor in this limbo's what I wish.

CAMILLA. Agreed. There's thunder that deserves to sing.

GENEVA. No thunder can be heard this morning, girls.

The sea of fog is shouting out nothing.

The world is scared to speak as silence curls.

VIOLA. She's yet to move, to walk away, to leave.

We've seen her back for minutes that abhor.

GENEVA. We'll wait and stand beside our grieving queen.

VIOLA. Distraught... who'll sign departure lists but her?

GENEVA. We'll sign it, then we'll say she signs it still

as in the Widow Ward our queen's distilled.

UNSEEN ANGELS. Before she woke, the angels rushed
and stole her like they stole him once.
Victorianry mansions blushed
as queens were led where widows cough.

NEVERRIA. Behind the bars, they all rehearse
and read their given lines aloud.
Beautifully reciting verse
that the guards love to hear pronounced.
A mom and dad, a stranger son.
The warden said invite the families.
They all arrive with suits and ties
because the prison's putting on a play.
The prison's putting on a play.
In matching suits, they face the pews
inside the prison's chapel upon the stage
where soliloquy speeches spew
because the prison's putting on a play.
The prison's putting on a play.

GENEVA. We told her that today's inspection day.
Behold her zombie pace, and zombie speech,
WILLOW. She paces in a damning mindless state
VIOLA. with arms prepared for Franco's ghost to reach.
WILLOW. Be stealthily throughout your quick exit.
The queen's my patient now. I'll watch her now.
I'll watch her pace until she's well again
VIOLA. if madness ever dares to settle down.
CAMILLA. This feels bizarre. I hate to leave her here.
GENEVA. Camilla, Neverria needs this break
until her craze of grief no longer blears.
CAMILLA. She paces in a mindful human state.
WILLOW. She's coming back, believing that she'll leave!
Farewell, you angels. Flee her zombie reach.

GENEVA. A charming bruise has grown as lovers lose.
She now embarks to go and chase a ghost,
with scarlet music notes of Love; her clues.
It's growing dark below her gaze of hope.
CAMILLA. She paces like the organ's yet to end,
with that zigzagging pattern floors abhor.
I hate to watch her hoping arms extend.
Perhaps she tracks to try and find his corpse.
VIOLA. His corpse has faded. No longer around.
I signed his name on the departure list.
CAMILLA. I guess it's up to us to sign it now.
GENEVA. Tonight, today, forever too I think.
CAMILLA. This limbo needs a queen; our puppet queen.
So fitting in this purgatory scene.

CAMILLA. Was Franco right about the modern day?

VIOLA. I think he wrecked too long to think correct.

It's done, despite his spill of auburn lakes.

CAMILLA. They ringed his neck to stop his wishing breath.

He stayed his course! It's human bravery.

As other men demand you slave for cash?

To slave and work for useless papery?

His hurricane of virtue stayed its path.

Viola, wait. My dear? Is that a tear?

VIOLA. A lot is weighing on my mindful scale.

I must release a weight, if just a tear,

and sob a day or two to ease the scale.

I think the miser's favorite color's green.

I wish they knew it; shades no brothers bleed.

CAMILLA. As mortals slaved for capital,
were warnings waking in his eyes?
Economically leashed with bills
they tried to gray his starry night.
A Lennon song, they put it on
and rocking back and forth inside their chairs.
Imaginary minds to waste.
If only people read his poetry.
If people read his poetry.
A dreaming boy. The misers' toy
to boss around inside a dull factory.
Another pawn to just employ.
If only people read his poetry.
If people read his poetry.

NEVERRIA. Franco fades ah- Franco fades away.
And like another Vincent Van Gogh,
I hope his poems and novels get to stay.
While making art, passion dug his grave-
so maddened that nobody read his poems.
UNSEEN ANGELS. Franco fades ah- Franco fades away.
NEVERRIA. He leaves behind an angel in his wake
who reaches out to hope to catch his ghost.
I hope his poems and novels get to stay.
Despite a miser rule, he went his way;
a boy who colored in a graying world.
UNSEEN ANGELS. Franco fades ah- Franco fades away.
NEVERRIA. It's always artists that they'll never tame.
With people on their- people on their phones,
I hope his poems and novels get to stay.
The pain a reading pair of eyes atone;
appreciating art will cure this woe.
I hope his poems and novels get to stay.
Franco fades ah- Franco fades away.

UNSEEN ANGELS. Our chorus moans for tragic shows,
and hopes this ends with true applause.
Will bittersweetly flowers grow?
He never was something he's not.
His empty room; a cluttered mess
with papers wondering why did he go.
An angel crowd will visit now.
Hear the angels talk about the artist?
Angels talk about the artist.
As people sat for media,
they all forgot about the ancient practice
because TV was easier.
Hear the angels talk about the artist?
Angels talk about the artist.